Judy Moody
Gets Famous!

Judy Moody & Gets Famous!

Megan McDonald

illustrated by
Peter Reynolds

SCHOLASTIC INC.

New York Toronto London Auckland Sydney
Mexico City New Delhi Hong Kong Buenos Aires

ISBN 0-439-37112-0

Text copyright © 2001 by Megan McDonald.
Illustrations copyright © 2001 by Peter Reynolds.
All rights reserved.
Published by Scholastic Inc., 555 Broadway, New York, NY 10012,
by arrangement with Candlewick Press.
SCHOLASTIC and associated logos are trademarks and/or
registered trademarks of Scholastic Inc.

12 11 10 9 8 7 6   3 4 5 6 7/0

Printed in the U.S.A.   40

First Scholastic printing, January 2002

This book was typeset in Stone Informal.

The illustrations were done in watercolor, tea, and milk.

For Kendra and Mary Lee
— M. M.
For Mum and Dad
— P. R.

Table of Contents

Judy

Roar!
Star of the show,
famous for her
many moods.

Who's Who

Dad

Judy's father.
Good at crossword
puzzles, quiz shows,
and garage sales.

Mom

Judy's mother.
Former glee club
member. Knows her
vegetables.

Stink

Judy's scene-stealing
younger brother and star
of the Moody Hall of Fame.

Mouse

Judy's cat.
Amazing contestant
in the Fur & Fangs
Famous Pet Contest.

Rocky

Judy's best friend
since FOREVER and
owner of a disappearing
Superman ring.

Mr. Todd

Judy's teacher,
a.k.a. Mr. Toad,
world's greatest
third-grade teacher.

Frank

Judy's paste-eating friend
and one quarter of a
human centipede.

Jessica

Judy's classmate,
Jessica *Aardwolf* Finch,
a.k.a. Know-it-all
Queen of the Spelling Bee.

How Do You Spell *Famous?*

Judy Moody marched into third grade on a plain old Thursday, in a plain old ordinary mood. That was *before* Judy got stung by the Queen Bee.

Judy sat down at her desk, in the front row next to Frank Pearl.

"Hey, did you see Jessica Finch?" asked Frank in a low voice.

"Yeah, so? I see her every day. She sits catty-cornered behind me."

"She's wearing a crown."

Judy turned to look at Jessica, then whispered to Frank, "Where'd she get that? Burger Barn?"

"I don't know," said Frank. "Ask her. She says it's bejeweled."

"Well, it looks be-dumb, if you ask me," said Judy, though secretly she admired the sparkling ruby-like gems.

"Hey, are those real rubies?" Judy asked Jessica.

"They're costume jewelry," Jessica said.

"Who are you dressing up as? The Queen of England?"

"No, I'm the Queen Bee," said Jessica. "I won the N. V. Spelling Bee on Saturday."

"The envy spelling bee?" Judy asked.

Judy didn't envy anybody who had to spell long words into a microphone with a million and one people staring bug-eyed at her. She knew those people were silently yelling *FLUB IT UP* because they wanted their own kid to win.

"Not *envy*. N. V. As in Northern Virginia."

"Oh," said Judy. "Is that where you got the crown?"

"It's a tiara," said Jessica. "T-I-A-R-A. A tiara is a fancy crown like the Queen of England wears. Queen of the Bee has to know tons of definitions."

"What word did you win for?" Judy asked. "Frank wants to know," she added, in case Jessica thought *she* was interested.

"*Artichoke.* It's a fourth-grade word."

Artichoke! Judy could barely spell *meat-loaf*! *Give me S-C-I-E-N-C-E any day*, she thought. Was that the rule? *I* before *E*? Or was it *E* before *I*?

"I have spelling posters in my room at home," said Jessica. "With all the rules. I even have a glow-in-the dark one."

"That would give me spelling night-mares. I'll take my glow-in-the-dark skele-ton poster any day. It shows all two hundred and six bones in the body!"

"Judy," said Mr. Todd. "The back of your head is not nearly as interesting as the front. And so far I've seen more of it today than I'd like."

"Sorry," said Judy, facing front again.

Jessica tapped Judy and passed her a folded page from the newspaper. Right there, SMACK-DAB in the MIDDLE of the newspaper for the whole world to see, was a picture of Jessica Finch. It even said LOCAL GIRL BECOMES QUEEN BEE in big fat headline letters.

"My dad says I got my fifteen minutes of fame," Jessica whispered to the back of Judy's head.

Judy did not turn around. She was green with N-V. Jessica A. Finch, Queen of the Dictionary, Class 3T, was famous! Judy could not help thinking how stupendous it would feel to be able to spell better than *meatloaf* and be the Queen Bee and wear a tiara. To get her own picture in the paper!

But she, Judy Moody, felt about as famous as a pencil.

◎　　◎　　◎

As soon as Judy got home from school, she decided to memorize the dictionary. But she got stuck on *aardwolf*. Three lousy words. Who ever heard of an aard*wolf* anyway? Silly old termite-eater. It had a pointy little head and beady little eyes and a pinched-up face that looked just like . . . Jessica A. Finch! Jessica *Aardwolf* Finch might be famous, but she was also a silly old termite-eater.

Since Jessica had become Queen Bee with the word *artichoke*, Judy decided to skip the dictionary and spell all the vegetables in the refrigerator instead.

"Do we have any artichokes?" Judy asked her mother, opening the door of the fridge.

"Since when did you start liking artichokes?" asked Mom.

"Don't worry, I'm not going to eat them or anything," said Judy. "It's for Spelling."

"Spelling?" Stink asked.

"Mr. Todd does have some creative ways of teaching Spelling," said Mom.

"Never mind," said Judy, giving up when she saw asparagus. Vegetables were too

hard to spell. There had to be a food g r o u p that was easier.

At dinner Judy slurped up a noodle and asked, "How do you spell *spaghetti*?"

"N-O-O-D-L-E," said Stink.

"S-P-A-G-H-E-T-T-I," said Dad.

"Or P-A-S-T-A," said Mom.

"Never mind," said Judy. "Please pass the B-R-E-A-D."

"How was school today?" Mom asked.

"W-E-L-L," Judy said. "Jessica Finch won a T-I-A-R-A in a spelling bee and got her picture in the P-A-P-E-R. Even if she does look like an A-A-R-D-W-O-L-F, aardwolf."

"So that's what all this spelling is about," said Mom.

"You're W-E-I-R-D," Stink told his sister.

"*I* comes before *E*, Stink. Except after *C*. Everybody knows *that*." What a meat-loaf.

"Actually," said Mom, "your brother's right."

"WHAT?" said Judy. "How can he be right? He broke the rule!"

"Lots of rules have exceptions," said Dad. "Times when you have to break the rule."

"No fair!" Judy slumped down in her chair. She was not going to become famous by spelling, that was for sure. The three strings of spaghetti left on her plate made the shape of a mean face. Judy made a mean face back.

Dad took a bite out of his garlic bread

and asked Judy, "You're not in one of your famous moods again, are you?"

The Moody Hall of Fame

The next day at breakfast, Judy ate her corn flakes without even spelling them.

There had to be lots of ways people got famous besides spelling.

While she munched, Judy watched her little brother, Stink, hang stuff up on the refrigerator: his report card, the self-portrait that made him look like a monkey, and a photo of himself in his flag costume, from the time he went to Washington, D. C.

without her. Above everything, he had spelled MOODY HALL OF FAME with letter magnets.

"Hey!" she said. "Where's me?"

"*I* made it," said Stink.

"Why not leave Judy some room, honey," said Mom. "She can hang things there too."

Judy ran back up the stairs, two by two. She searched her desk for things to put in the Moody Hall of Fame. But all she could find were rumpled-up papers, acorn hats, a year-old candy heart that said HOT STUFF, and a drawer full of pink dust from all the times she had erased her spelling words and brushed them into her top drawer.

She rummaged through her closet next. All she had there were her collections: Band-Aids, fancy toothpicks, body parts (from dolls!), Bazooka Joe comics, pizza tables. Forget it. A person could not be in a hall of fame for toothpicks and Band-Aids.

Then Judy remembered her scrapbox. Most kids, like Stink, had a scrapbook. What Judy had was a shoebox that smelled like old rubber. She stood on a chair and lifted the box down from the top shelf.

A lock of baby hair! A tooth she lost in first grade. Mom and Dad would never let her hang dead hair up on the fridge. And nobody wanted to see an old yellow tooth every time they opened the refrigerator. Judy came across a macaroni picture of herself in kindergarten, with a screaming O for a mouth. She put it back. Stink would just love the chance to call her a noodle head. And remind her that she had a big mouth.

Where were her report cards? There had to be some good ones. Certificates? Blue ribbons? She must have won something, sometime. But all she found were baby footprints, half-melted birthday candles, and dopey drawings of people with four eyes that she'd scribbled in preschool.

What about pictures of herself?

Pictures! Judy flipped through some old photos in an envelope. She had to find something as good as the picture of Stink the time he met the president. Here she

was with Santa Claus. But Santa looked like he was snoring. And there she was standing next to Abraham Lincoln (cardboard). No way could she be in the Moody Hall of Fame for having her picture taken with a cardboard president.

Then there was the one where she was facedown on the neighbor's driveway, throwing a tantrum, because she did NOT want to get her picture taken.

It was no use. Judy could not think of a single thing famous enough for the Moody Hall of Fame.

Judy went back down to the kitchen. The letter magnets on the fridge should have said THE STINK HALL OF FAME.

"So? Where's your stuff?" Stink asked.

"Did you leave it upstairs or something?"

"Or something," said Judy. She hadn't even found the crummy old ribbon from the time she won the Viola Swamp Look-Alike Contest in first grade.

"Mom?" Judy asked. "Did you ever get your picture in the paper?"

"Sure," said Mom. "Lots of times. For the high school glee club."

"What's *glee*?" asked Stink.

"*Glee* means being happy," Mom told him, "or cheerful."

"They put your picture in the paper just for being happy?" asked Judy.

"No." Mom laughed. "Glee club is a singing group." Judy did not think anybody would take *her* picture just for being happy.

Or for singing songs about it.

"How about you, Dad?" asked Judy.

"They said my name on the radio once for having the right answer to a quiz-show question."

"What was the question?" asked Stink.

"How many presidents were born in Virginia?"

"How many?" asked Stink and Judy.

"Eight."

"Wow," said Judy.

"Aren't you going to ask me?" asked Stink.

"You never had your picture in the paper," said Judy.

"Yes, I did, didn't I, Mom?" Stink asked. "It's in my baby scrapbook."

"You've heard that story, Judy, about how we waited too long to leave for the hospital and your brother was born in the back of the Jeep."

"I was even on TV! On the news!"

"Oh, yeah," said Judy. "Thanks for reminding me."

It wasn't fair. Her own stinky brother got to be on the real live news. She, Judy Moody, was not even famous enough for the refrigerator.

Infamous

Rocky was already waiting for them at the manhole.

"Hey, Rock," said Stink, "did you ever get your picture in the paper?"

"Sure," said Rocky. "Bunches of times."

"You did?" asked Judy.

"No, not really," said Rocky. "But they did hang my picture up in the library one time."

"See?" Judy said to Stink. "Even my best friend is famous."

"Why'd they hang your picture up in the library?" asked Stink.

"My mom took me to the library to see this magician guy, you know? He did this trick where he took my Superman ring and made it disappear. Then he pulled it out of his sleeve along with a bunch of scarves. They took a picture of it and I'm the kid in the front row with my eyes bugging out. Not exactly famous."

"Still," said Judy.

When Judy got to school, Mr. Todd said, "Let's go over our spelling words." Spelling, spelling, spelling. The whole wide world was hung up on spelling.

Judy leaned over and whispered to Frank. "Hey, Frank, ever had your picture in the paper?"

"It's no big deal," said Frank. "I was three years old."

Adam stood up and spelled the word, "R-E-C-Y-C-L-E."

"What was it for?" whispered Judy.

Hailey stood up and spelled the word, "I-C-I-C-L-E."

"I won the Grandpa Grape Coloring Contest in the newspaper. You had to color this dancing grape cartoon guy. He used to be on grape juice. I couldn't even stay in the lines."

Randi stood up and spelled, "M-O-T-O-R-C-Y-C-L-E."

Even Frank Pearl was famous. For scribbling on a dancing grape.

"Everybody I know is F-A-M-O-U-S," Judy grumped.

"Judy," said Mr. Todd, "were you hoping to get a white card today?"

A white card! Three white cards in one

week meant you had to stay after school! She already had two. And it was only Wednesday.

"Why don't you spell the bonus word aloud for us?" Mr. Todd said.

Bonus word? thought Judy. She hadn't been paying attention. She, Judy Moody, was in a pickle. Pickle? Was that the word? "Could I have the definition please?" she asked.

The whole class cracked up. "It's something you eat," said Rocky.

Judy stood up. "P-O-P-S-I-C-L-E. *Popsicle*," she announced confidently.

"Very good," said Mr. Todd. "For *popsicle*. Unfortunately that wasn't our bonus spelling word for today."

"Jessica? Would you like to spell the word for the class?"

Jessica Finch stood up tall, holding her pointy head so she looked very queenly. "P-U-M-P-E-R-N-I-C-K-E-L. *Pumpernickel*," said Jessica, faster than necessary.

Pumpernickel was one of those artichokey kind of words that only Pinch Face herself could spell. *I bet she can't spell* aardwolf, thought Judy.

"Judy," Mr. Todd said, "if you study your spelling words and pay attention in class, you can avoid getting white cards and we'll both get along famously."

There it was again. *That word.*

It was almost time for Science, her best subject, so it would be easy for Judy to pay attention. She'd sit up straight and raise her hand a bunch, like Jessica Finch.

She, Judy Moody, would *not* get another white card.

❧   ❧   ❧

Judy studied the squirming worm on her desk up close.

"As you all know," said Mr. Todd, "we've been raising mealworms. Today I'm passing one out for each of you to examine. You can often find mealworms at home. Where do you think you would find them in your house?"

Judy raised her hand.

"They like to eat oatmeal and flour and stuff," she said when Mr. Todd called on her.

"So maybe in your kitchen?"

"Right. Good," said Mr. Todd. "They are actually the larvae of a type of beetle. The flour beetle. Mealworms are nocturnal," said Mr. Todd. "Who can explain what that means?"

Judy's hand shot up again.

"Judy?"

"They sleep in the day and wake up at night," said Judy.

"Fine," said Mr. Todd. "This kind of mealworm is called a *T. molitor.* Everyone take a minute and count how many segments you find on your mealworm. Then write it down in your notebook."

Judy counted thirteen segments, not

including the head. She wrote it in her note-book right away. While she waited for the next question, she let the mealworm climb up her finger. She let it climb up her pencil. Rare! The mealworm perched on her eraser.

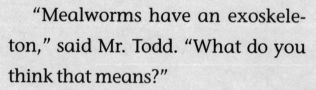

"Mealworms have an exoskele-ton," said Mr. Todd. "What do you think that means?"

Judy knew everything about bones and skeletons. Inside ones and out. She knew the answer again. Judy shot her hand straight up in the air. Judy forgot about the pencil in her hand. She forgot about the meal-worm on the tip of her eraser.

Mr. Todd called on Rocky.

Judy watched her mealworm fly through the air. She watched it land smack-dab on Jessica Finch. She watched it crawl up the front of Jessica's shirt and right up onto the tip of Jessica's ponytail.

Judy forgot all about the white card. She waved her hand wildly at Jessica until Jessica looked up, then pointed frantically at Jessica's head.

"*Aaagh!*" Jessica screamed worse than a hyena and flicked her hair to shake off the mealworm. *T. molitor* sailed through the air, hit the chalkboard, and fell to the floor. Class 3T went wild.

"Class!" said Mr. Todd, clapping his hands. "Everybody quiet down. Jessica," he

said. "I'll not have anybody throwing meal-worms in my classroom." He wrote her name on the board.

"But I didn't . . . it was . . . she did! . . ."

"That's enough. See me after Science for a white card."

Jessica glared squinty-eyed at Judy. Her pointy ears looked pointier. Her pinched-up face looked even pinchier. Judy faced front.

Judy knew it was all her own fault. But she did not want to get a third white card.

Jessica Finch probably never got a white card before, thought Judy. She probably didn't even know before today what it felt like to get in trouble. All Jessica had was one puny little white card, and one puny little white card never hurt anybody.

For the rest of the morning, Judy felt more and more like a bug. No, a louse.

After lunch, her neck started to itch. Then her elbow. She scratched her left knee. Her toe itched inside her shoe.

By the end of the day, Judy went to talk to her teacher. "Mr. Todd," she asked, scratching her ankle, "do you think not telling the truth can make a person itch?" *Scratch, scratch, scratch.*

"I think so," said Mr. Todd. "Is there something you're itching to tell me?"

"Yes," said Judy. *Scratch, scratch.* "In Science today?" *Scratch.* "It was my mealworm." *Scratch.* "My fault."

Scratch, scratch. "Not Jessica Finch's."

Judy told the whole truth.

"Thank you," said Mr. Todd. "I appreciate your coming to me with the truth, Judy. I know that's not always easy."

"Does this mean I don't have to get a third white card?"

"I'm afraid not," said Mr. Todd. "I still want you to learn to pay better attention."

Mr. Todd erased Jessica's name on the board and wrote Judy's name in its place. Judy hung her head.

"Honestly, it's not so bad staying after school with me. We'll find something useful to do, okay? Like maybe clean out the fish tank."

"Mr. Todd, is there a word for somebody

who gets famous for all the wrong rea-
sons?" asked Judy.

"Yes," said Mr. Todd. "That would be . . .
infamous."

Fame Is the Pits

Judy peeled a banana.

"Can I have that?" asked Stink. Judy handed him the banana peel.

"Not *that*!" said Stink.

Judy took a monster bite, then handed Stink the banana. She picked up a cherry instead.

"What are you writing?" she asked her dad, popping the cherry into her mouth.

"Garage sale," said Dad. "I'm running an ad in the paper. It's time to get rid of all that old stuff out there."

"Old stuff?" asked Judy, perking up. Old stuff got people in the newspaper. Really really old stuff even got people on TV. "What old stuff?"

"Your old bike, Mom's books from college, Stink's baby clothes."

"Don't we have any old-old stuff?"

"There's Dad," said Stink.

"Thanks a lot," said Dad.

"No. I mean like Cleopatra's eyelash," said Judy. "Or a hammer used to build the Statue of Liberty. You know. Stuff old enough to be really worth something."

"Stuff you didn't know you had and you find out you're rich?" Stink grinned. "Like antiques from your great-great-great-grandmother? You go on TV and they tell you it's worth a bunch of money."

"I'm afraid nobody's going to get rich around here. Our old stuff is junk," said Dad.

"ROAR," said Judy. She pulled the stem off another cherry.

If only she had something unusual. Really rare. Like maybe a broken plate from another century, or an old letter from the American Revolution.

"So, what's happening in school these days?" Dad asked.

Judy sat up. Had Dad heard about the white cards? "What do you mean?"

"I mean, is anything interesting going on?"

"Can I stay after school Friday?" asked Judy. "Mr. Todd says I can help clean the fish tank."

"P-U," said Stink.

"We'll see if Mom can pick you up. How about you, Stink?"

Judy popped another cherry into her mouth.

"We learned this funny story about George Washington," said Stink. "It's about not telling a lie."

Judy chomped down on the cherry.

"See, he chopped down this cherry tree. And when his dad asked who did it, Washington said, 'I cannot tell a lie.' And he told on himself."

Judy almost choked. She spit out her cherry pit. It went zinging across the table at Stink.

"Hey," said Stink. "She spit at me."

"It was an accident," said Judy.

"Judy!" said Dad.

"Okay. Okay. I cannot tell a lie. I coughed a cherry pit at Stink."

"Pick up the cherry pit," said Dad.

Judy reached under Stink's chair and picked it up off the floor.

"No fair," said Judy. "Why should anyone

get famous for telling a lie? The whole story about the lie is a lie!"

"Most people don't realize it's not true," said Dad.

"It's still a good story," said Stink.

Judy turned the cherry pit over and over. It gave her a brilliant Judy-Moody-Gets-Famous idea. A two-hundred-fifty-year-old idea.

Judy took the cherry pit upstairs to her room. She got out her hair dryer, and turned it on HIGH.

"What are you doing?" asked Stink, who had followed her upstairs.

"What does it look like?" said Judy. "I'm blow-drying my cherry pit."

"You're nuts," said Stink.

After he left, Judy got out the tiny hammer from her doctor kit, the one for testing reflexes. She tapped on the cherry pit to give it scars, so it would look old. Very, very old. Next she took a pin and carved the initials GW on the bottom. Then, she took out her clear plastic bug-box, the one with the magnifying glass on top, and put the cherry pit inside for safekeeping, initials-side up.

"Rare!" said Judy. And that was the truth.

◎   ◎   ◎

On the afternoon of the garage sale, Stink had his own table filled with tub toys, rusty Matchbox cars, Lincoln Logs, a rubber band ball, Shrinky Dinks that had already been shrunk, paper cooties, broken rhythm instruments, and glow-in-the-dark bugs he made with his Creepy Crawlers machine.

Matchbox cars   Lincoln Logs   Glow-in-the-dark bugs

"Stink, nobody is going to buy that stuff," Judy told him.

"Yeah, right," said Stink. "And they're going to buy air?" he said, pointing to Judy's empty table.

"You'll see," said Judy. "I have something better than junk." She covered her table with a midnight blue tablecloth that looked like velvet. She put up a sign:

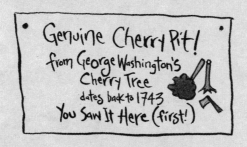

Genuine Cherry Pit!
from George Washington's
Cherry Tree
dates back to 1743
You Saw It Here (first!)

Then she set her magnifying bug-box in the middle of the table. Inside was — *ta da!* — the FAMOUS cherry pit.

Judy added one more line to her sign:

5¢ A LOOK

She could hardly sit still. She wondered how long it would take the newspaper people to come take her picture with the two-hundred-fifty-year-old cherry pit.

Little kids put a nickel in the can and said, "Wow, is that REALLY from George Washington's cherry tree?"

"I cannot tell a lie," said Judy. "It is!"

"Where'd you get it?" they asked.

"It's been in the family forever."

"Forever since last week," said Stink. Judy turned on him with her stinging caterpillar look.

"How do you know it's really George Washington's?" they asked.

"Just look," said Judy. She opened the lid and lifted out the cherry pit. "It says GW right here. See?"

"Let me see," said a girl named Hannah. She showed her little brother. "GW. It's just like M&M's."

"M&M's!" said the boy, and popped the pit into his mouth.

"Ricky, NO!" said his older sister. But it was too late.

"Spit!" said Judy.

"Spit it out, Ricky!" said Hannah.

Ricky gulped!

"Oh, no! Did he swallow it?" asked Judy. "Stick your finger in his mouth. Is it still in there?"

"It's gone," said Hannah. "Say you're sorry, Ricky."

"M&M's. Yum," said Ricky.

"This is the pits," said Judy. "Now what am I going to do when the newspaper comes?"

"Duh. Make another one?" said Stink.

Judy groaned. Judy moaned. In one gulp, that kid had swallowed her famous two-hundred-fifty-year-old George Washington cherry pit. In one gulp, Ricky the neighbor kid had swallowed Judy Moody's ticket to fame.

The only picture of *that* cherry pit would be an x-ray.

Famous Pet Contest

Stink counted his garage sale money at the kitchen table. *Clink. Clink. CLINK.*

"Stink, you're counting that money out loud on purpose," said Judy.

"I can't help it!" said Stink. "Mom, tell her. Money makes noise. When you have so much of it." He grinned.

Judy crumpled up the newspaper that had their garage sale ad in it. She stuffed it angrily into the trash.

"Recycle, please," said Mom.

"Whoa," said Stink. "The recycle queen put paper in the trash?"

"Can I use it to line Mouse's litter box?" asked Judy.

"Good idea," said Mom.

Judy uncrumpled the paper and spread it on the floor to flatten it.

EARLY BIRD SPECIAL! . . .

GARAGE DOOR SALE! . . .

FAMOUS PET CONTEST! . . .

KISS BAD BREATH GOOD-BYE!

Wait! Did that say *famous*? Judy went back and read it again:

FAMOUS PET CONTEST

Bring your pet to
FUR & FANGS
this Saturday!

Enter your pet in our
famous pet-trick contest!

Have fun! Win prizes!

Winners will receive a
blue ribbon, a gift certificate,
and get their picture
published in the
NORTHERN VIRGINIA STAR!

Judy could not believe her eyes. "Where's Mouse?" she asked. "Upstairs," said Mom.

"Here, Mousey, Mousey," Judy called. Mouse came down the stairs and strolled into the kitchen, looking for some lunch.

Judy scooped up her cat and kissed her on the nose: *"Mww, mww, mwww.* You, the

best, most wonderful cat in the whole wide world with tuna fish on top, are going to make *me* famous!"

Visions of blue ribbons and certificates with fancy writing danced in her head. "*And* I get my picture in the paper."

"Hey," she said to her family, "does anybody feel like a piece of toast?"

❂   ❂   ❂

When Judy hurried into Fur & Fangs with Mouse and Stink that Saturday, it was packed.

Clutching a piece of bread, she said, "Everyone in the entire state of Virginia must own a pet that can do a trick. Hey, there's Frank!"

"And there's Rocky," said Stink.

"You guys! Frank! Rocky! Over here!" Judy called.

Frank's dog, Sparky, sniffed a purple dog bone. Sparky sniffed Judy's ankle. Sparky sniffed a ferret.

"What trick does Sparky do?" Stink asked Frank.

"He jumps through a Hula-Hoop, don't you, boy?" said Frank.

"I brought Houdini," Rocky said, showing them his iguana. "If you scare him, like with a loud noise or something, he can make the end of his tail drop right off."

"Rare," said Judy.

She looked around at all the other pets. There was a rabbit and a turtle, a white rat named Elvis, and a striped salamander.

Judy saw a hamster racing on a wheel, a snake so still it looked fake, and a shell that was supposed to be a hermit crab. Someone had even brought a stuffed monkey.

"Time for the contest!" yelled the pet store lady over all the squeaking and squawking, growling and yowling.

All the people with pets formed a circle. First was a dancing cricket. Then a turtle that rolled over and a rabbit that drank from a straw.

Polly the parrot sang the first five notes of "The Star-Spangled Banner." Judy caught herself clapping.

When it was Frank's turn, Sparky jumped through the Hula-Hoop three times and everybody clapped. Then Rocky could not get Houdini's tail to drop off. "Dogs make him nervous," Rocky explained.

Three pet tricks later, Polly was still singing.

Emily from school had a ferret named Suzy who brushed its own teeth. Stink liked it the best.

"But all it did was eat the toothpaste," said Judy.

When it was Judy's turn, she set up a toaster on the floor, dropped a piece of bread into the slot, then took Mouse out of her cat carrier.

"This is Mouse," Judy told the audience. "She's going to make toast." The audience clapped. Judy stood Mouse on the table. "Don't be nervous," she whispered.

Mouse sat down and began licking her paw.

"Look at the toaster, Mouse," whispered Judy. "The toaster!" Judy pushed it toward Mouse.

Mouse swatted the toaster. Mouse swiped at the toaster. Mouse pushed the toaster away with her paw. Everybody cracked up. Judy held out a Tasty Tuna Treat. Mouse stood up. Mouse saw herself in the toaster!

Judy held her breath.

Mouse swiped at the toaster one more time. This time she pressed down the button with her paw. The slice of bread disappeared! The red coils heated up.

The crowd got quiet. A minute later, the toast popped up.

"Ta da!" called Judy.

"Hooray!" Everybody clapped and cheered.

"Mouse, I'll be famous at last!" Judy squeezed her.

"And now, last but not least," said the pet store lady, "a chicken that plays the piano."

Up stepped David, a boy with a chicken on a leash.

"This is Mozart," said the boy. Mozart pecked out three notes on the toy piano with his beak. "'Three Blind Mice!'" some-one yelled. The crowd went wild.

Judy felt a familiar twinge, the tug of a bad mood. She, Judy Moody, would never

be as famous as a piano-playing chicken.

For the grand finale, everyone paraded their pets, marching in a circle.

"What a great contest this year," said the pet store lady. "I'd like to thank all of you for coming. Now, for the prizes," said the pet store lady. "If I call your pet's name, please step into the center of the circle."

A man stepped up to the circle with a big camera.

"The newspaper! They're here," Judy announced.

"In third place, Suzy Chang, the tooth-brushing ferret."

Please-please-please, Judy wished silently.

"Second place is Mouse Moody, the cat who makes toast!"

"That's you!" said Frank and Rocky, pushing Judy into the circle.

"Mouse, we won!" cried Judy. "Second place!" At last her time had come. At last her chance to be famous.

"And first prize goes to Mozart Puckett, the piano-playing chicken! Let's hear it for all the famous pets!"

The crowd went wild. Each pet got a blue ribbon to wear and a gift certificate to Fur & Fangs. The winners lined up to have a picture taken! Judy was on the end, holding Mouse, but Mouse squirmed and leaped out of Judy's arms. Flash! Judy blinked. The newspaper man snapped a picture faster than lightning.

"Thank you, everybody! That's it!" yelled the pet store lady.

"That's it?" asked Judy.

Judy's fifteen minutes of fame lasted only fifteen seconds. Fifteen seconds of fame, and she, Judy Moody, had blinked.

◉　　◉　　◉

The following morning, Judy ran outside to fetch the paper. She whipped through the pages. Her heart beat faster.

"Here it is!" Judy cried. She could not believe her eyes. There were David Puckett and Emily Chang with mile-wide smiles. There were Mozart the chicken and Suzy the ferret.

"Let me see!" said Stink. "Hey, there's Mouse!"

"I'm not even in the picture!" yelled Judy.

"There you are!" said Stink, pointing to an elbow.

"I'm not famous!" Judy wailed. "I'm an elbow!"

"Let's see," said Dad. He read the caption. "Blah-blah, *winners of the Famous Pet Contest,* blah-blah. It says your name, right here. See? *Mouse and Judy . . . Muddy.*"

"WHAT!" said Judy. "*Muddy*? Let me see."

"Judy Muddy! That's a good one," said Stink.

"Judy Muddy! No one will ever know it's me," said Judy.

"We'll know," said Dad.

Judy frowned. "I guess your name is Mud," Dad said, laughing.

"ROAR!" said Judy.

"At least it says Mouse won the contest," Mom said. She cut out the picture and hung it up on the fridge.

"Great," said Judy. "Even my cat's in the Moody Hall of Fame."

Mom kissed the top of Judy's head. "And you have one very famous elbow."

Broken Records

Judy studied her famous elbow in the mirror. She squished her elbow into a wrinkled happy face. She squinched her elbow into a mad face.

If Judy ever hoped to be more famous than an elbow, she needed some help. Judy called all members of the Toad Pee Club. "Meet at the clubhouse," she told everybody.

Rocky, Frank, and Judy crowded into the blue tent in her backyard. Last was Stink, who carried Toady, their mascot, in one hand, and walked while reading a book.

"Stink, you better watch out or you'll renew your membership."

"OH!" said Stink. He tossed Toady into the bucket before the toad famous for peeing in people's hands did it again.

"Now," said Judy, "how can we make me famous?"

"Let's think," Rocky said.

"Stink, you're not thinking," said Judy.

"Getting famous is boring," said Stink, leafing through his book.

"Stink, what book could be soooooooooo interesting?"

Stink held up the *Guinness Book of World Records*. Judy looked at Frank. Frank looked at Rocky. Rocky looked at Judy. "Brain-storm!" the three yelled at the same time. Then they cracked up.

"Stink, you are a genius. The secret to getting famous is right there in your hands."

Stink checked his hands.

"Don't you get it?" said Judy. "I could break a record and get in that book! Then I'd be superfamous."

"Famous. Famous. Famous. YOU are a broken record," Stink told her.

"Hardee-har-har," said Judy.

"You know how you collect stuff, like

Band-Aids?" said Frank. "You could break a record for collecting something. Like the most pizza tables."

"Or scabs!" said Judy.

"*Bluck*," said Stink. "There's a guy in here who collects throw-up bags from airplanes. He has two thousand one hundred and twelve. One bag even has a connect-the-dots drawing of Benjamin Franklin on it."

"That's way better than scabs," said Judy.

"Hey, look," Rocky said, reading over Stink's shoulder. "World's longest word. Spell that and you could be the next Jessica Finch."

The word was: *Pneumonoultramicroscopicsilicovocanoconiosis.*

"Whoa. Forty-five letters," said Frank, counting.

"Not even Queen Bee herself could spell that!" said Judy.

"It says here it's an ucky disease from volcanoes," Rocky said. "No lie."

"Wait! I got it. There's a guy in here with the longest neck," said Stink. "We could all pull on your head to stretch your neck out!"

"I want to be famous, not a giraffe," said Judy.

"With a giraffe neck you would be famous," Stink told her.

"Let me see that book." Judy grabbed the book of records and flipped through the pages. Longest gum wrapper chain? It took thirty-one years to make! Longest fingernail? No way; the guy hasn't cut his thumbnail since 1952. Best spitter? Judy could spit.

Then she saw it. Right there on page 399.

The human centipede!

"Okay. Listen up. We're going to be a giant creepy-crawly," said Judy. "Let's tie our shoelaces together, then walk like a caterpillar. The old record is ninety-eight feet and five inches. Rocky, remember last summer we measured with a string? It was one hundred feet to your house and back. So all we have to do is walk from here to Rocky's and back to break the record."

They sat in a line, one behind the other,

like desks in a row. First Judy, then Frank, Rocky, and Stink.

"Hey, I'm always last!" said Stink.

"You're the rear end," said Judy.

"Tie one shoelace to the person in front, and one to the person in back," she called.

"How are we ever going to stand up?" asked Stink.

"On the count of three," Judy began. "One, two . . ." Judy took the first step. Frank's foot shot up and out from under him. Like bowling pins, Frank toppled sideways, Rocky fell over on his ear, and Stink crashed on his elbows.

Frank snorted first. Rocky cracked up so bad he sprayed everybody.

"Hic-CUP!" said Stink.

When they were finally standing, without anybody falling or snorting or hiccupping, they each tried to take a step. One . . . two . . . three.

"The human centipede!" called Judy. She pictured the human centipede in her imagination—growing longer and longer, all wiggly and squiggly with tons of legs, and she, Judy Moody, at the head with biting fangs and poison claws!

"*Hsss!*" said Judy.

"No hopping, Rocky," called Frank.

"My lace is all twisted," said Rocky.

"Hold up!" yelled Stink from the end of the line.

That's when it happened.

Judy stopped, but the rest of the centipede kept going! They all began to fall. *Crunch!* Judy stepped on Frank's hand. Frank's other arm socked Rocky in the stomach. Stink's foot landed in Rocky's hair.

Three steps, and they had crumbled into a human pretzel.

"Hey! Watch it!" Stink yelled.

"I'm all twisted," Rocky said.

"OWWWWWWWWWWWWW!" Frank screamed. Frank was holding up his right arm with his left hand.

Frank Pearl's right pinky finger looked all floppy. It looked all floopy. Frank Pearl's pinky was twice as fat as normal and dangled down the wrong way.

"OOOH! What happened?" asked Judy.

"It hurts . . . bad," said Frank, tears streaming down his face. "Real bad."

"Stink, run and get Mom. Fast!"

What if Judy had broken a finger, not a record? If Frank's pinky was broken, it was all Judy's fault.

Judy no longer felt like a human centipede. She, Judy Moody, felt more like a human *worm*.

Broken Parts

"So which one of you's the patient?" asked a tall man with a red beard in a long white coat.

Frank held up his little blue sausage of a finger.

"Ouch!" said the man. "How'd this happen?"

Frank looked over at Judy. Judy stared a hole in the carpet.

"We were playing," Frank answered.

"We were making a human centipede so my sister could be famous!" said Stink. "And she stepped on Frank!"

Judy sent Stink her best troll-eyes stare, complete with stinging-caterpillar eyebrows. The man laughed. "Okay. Well. I'm Ron, the emergency-room nurse. I'll take you back, and the doctor's gonna fix you right up, Frank. Is your mom or dad here?"

"My mom went to call Frank's mom," said Judy.

"Okay. Tell you what. The children's wing is right through those red doors. Why don't you two wait in the playroom there. It'll be more fun. I'll tell your mom you're there, when she comes back."

Too bad Rocky went home. Now she was

stuck with Stink. They pushed through the red doors and into a long hallway. At the end of the hall was a room marked THE MAGIC PLAYROOM. Judy and Stink went in.

The walls were papered with teddy bears in hospital gowns, holding balloons. Each bear had crutches or bandages or sat in a wheelchair. There was a couch, a table with crayons and paper for coloring, a plastic castle, and a bookshelf with books about going to the hospital. There was even a miniature operating table on wheels. The only kid in the playroom was a girl in a wheelchair.

"How come you're in a wheelchair?" Stink asked her.

"Stink, you shouldn't ask stuff like that."

"It's okay," said the girl. "I got a new heart. They can't let me walk around yet. They have to keep me at the hospital for a long, long time to make sure it works."

"A whole new heart! Wow!" said Stink. "What's wrong with your old one?"

"Stink!" said Judy, even though she wanted to know too.

"It broke, I guess," said the girl.

"Were you scared?" Judy asked.

The girl nodded. "Guess what. My scar goes from my neck all the way down to my bellybutton."

"What's your name?" asked Stink.

"Laura," said the girl.

"That's one brave heart you got there, Laura," said Judy.

"Daddy says I'm a brave girl," Laura said. "I'm getting a hamster when I go home. Do you have a hamster?"

"No," said Judy. "I have a cat named Mouse."

"There's nothing to do here," said Laura, looking around.

"They have doctor stuff," said Judy.

"Look! A real sling and stuff!" said Stink, kneeling next to a big cardboard box. He pulled out Ace bandages, boxes of gauze, and tongue depressors. Even a stethoscope and a pair of crutches.

"Stink, can I put your arm in a sling?" Judy asked.

"No way," said Stink.

"How about you, Laura? I know how. For real."

"I'm sick of doctor stuff," Laura said.

"What about dolls?" Stink asked. "There's a bunch of dolls in this box."

"They all have broken arms and legs, or no heads," Laura said. "And some of them have cancer."

"What do you mean?" Judy asked.

"They're bald, like Sarah, in my same room."

"That's not fair," Judy said. "They should at least have dolls to play with that aren't sick."

The nurse came back just then. "Time to go back to your room," she told Laura. "Did you kids meet our brave girl?"

"Yes!" said Judy and Stink.

"I hope your new heart works great!" said Judy, as Laura left with the nurse.

"Bye!" called Stink.

Judy looked through the doll box. Laura was right. All the dolls were dirty or broken or hairless or headless.

Mrs. Moody poked her head in the door-way. "Hello!"

"Mom!" said Stink.

"Is Frank okay?" Judy asked.

"His finger's broken," said Mrs. Moody, "but his mom is with him now. He's getting a splint."

"Rare! A real splint!" said Judy.

"He won't be playing any basketball for a while, but he's going to be just fine. So. Ready to go?"

Stink and Judy followed Mrs. Moody out of the playroom. Halfway down the hall, Judy stopped, holding Stink back by his shirt.

"Stink," she said so her mom couldn't hear. "Give me your backpack."

"What?"

"Your backpack. I need it." Stink made a face and handed over the pack.

"Catch up with Mom and tell her I forgot something. I'll be right back."

Judy dashed back into the playroom and over to the box of broken dolls. Looking around to make sure no one was coming, she stuffed the dolls into the backpack. Judy zipped it shut, flung it over her shoulder like a lumpy Santa Claus sack, and headed back down the hall.

When Mom stopped to ask a question at the desk, Stink asked, "Hey! What's in there?"

"Nothing."

"Nothing does not make a big fat lump.

Did you take that doctor stuff? You took stuff! You stole! I'm telling!"

"Shh! You can't tell anybody, Stink, or we'll get in trouble for stealing."

"We? You mean *you'll* get in trouble," said Stink. "Are you crazy? Do you want to be famous for being the only third grader who ever went to jail?"

"Swear you won't tell, Stink."

"What will you give me?"

"I'll let you look at real spit under my microscope."

"Okay. I swear."

"You swore!" said Judy. "I'm telling."

Body Parts

As soon as Judy got home, she unloaded the backpack and spread the dolls out on her bottom bunk. She, Doctor Judy Moody, was in an operating mood. On her bed was a doll that didn't talk or cry anymore, and one with no arms. There was a headless doll, and one that was bald.

First Judy gave each of the dolls a bath.

"I know just what I need," said Judy.

"Body parts!" She dug out her collection: long arms, skinny arms, brown legs, pink legs, middles with bellybuttons, one bare foot, a thing that looked like a neck, and all sorts of heads—small heads, fat heads, Barbie heads, bald heads! Judy emptied a whole bag of body parts onto her bed. "Rare!"

Judy glued a red wig with yarn braids onto the doll with no hair and gave another one arms that bent. Judy bent the arm back and forth, back and forth, to test it out. "Boo!" said the doll each time Judy lifted her arm.

"You don't scare me!" Judy told the doll.

"And for you," she said to the headless

doll. "A new head!" From all the heads on her bed, Judy chose one with brown hair and green eyes.

"There you go," said Judy, popping on the new head. But when she turned the doll upside down to put some shoes on her, the doll's head flew off and bounced across the floor!

"Whoa!" said Judy, running after the head. "That won't work. Let's try this one. How would you like eyes that can close and open?" Judy twisted the new head onto the doll's neck and waved her up, down, up, down through the air a few times to watch the eyes open and close.

"Voilà!" said Judy. She kissed the doll right on the nose.

Next she dressed each doll in a blue-and-white hospital gown she made from an old sheet, and gave each of them a paper bracelet printed with a name: Colby, Molly, Suzanna, Laura.

"Knock, knock," called Stink, pounding on her door.

"Go away," said Judy.

"Knock, knock!" said Stink.

"Who's there?" said Judy.

"I, Stink," said Stink.

"I Stink who?"

"I stink you should let me in your room," said Stink, letting himself in anyway. He peeked behind the blanket hanging over the bottom bunk.

"*Aaagh!*" he yelled, jumping back in shock. "Those dolls! The hospital—you stole! Those are . . . those aren't . . . if Mom and Dad find out . . ."

"Stink, you *promised* you wouldn't tell."

"Yeah, but . . ."

Judy was making a tiny cast out of oogey

wet newspaper. "Look, if you keep quiet, I'll let you help me."

"It's a deal!" said Stink.

Stink and Judy finished putting the cast on one of the doll's legs. When it dried, they painted it white and signed it with lots of made-up names. After that, they made a sling for another doll, with a scrap of cloth. On a different doll Doctor Judy put tattoo Band-Aids from her Band-Aid collection all over its legs, arms, and stomach.

"Double cool!" said Stink.

Last but not least was a rag doll made of cloth. Judy took a pink marker and drew a scar from the doll's neck down to her belly-button. Then she drew a red heart, broken in two. With black thread, she stitched the broken heart back together, hiding it under the doll's hospital gown.

"Just like that girl Laura!" Stink said.

When she was finished, Judy propped up all the dolls in a row on her bottom bunk and stood back to admire her work. She set her own doll, Hedda-Get-Betta, next to them.

"Wow, you made them look really good!" said Stink.

A little later Judy packed all the dolls into a box and secretly mailed them back to the hospital. Without a return address, no one would ever know that she was the one who had stolen the dolls.

It's like a real doll hospital, thought Judy. She, Judy Moody, was on her way to being just like First Woman Doctor, Elizabeth Blackwell.

Judy Moody and Jessica Flinch

On Monday morning Mr. Todd asked, "Where's Frank today?"

"Absent," said Judy.

"Oh, that's right. I heard that he broke his finger. Does anybody know how it happened?"

"It's a loooooooooooooooooooong story," said Judy.

"As long as a centipede!" said Rocky.

"I heard Judy Moody stepped on him!"

said Adam. "CRACK!" He bent his finger back like it was breaking.

"Okay, okay. We'll ask Frank all about it when he gets back."

"He'll be back tomorrow," Judy said.

Judy looked at the empty desk next to her. Without Frank, there was no one to snort at her jokes. Without Frank, she spelled *barnacle* with an *i*. Without Frank, she had nobody to tease about eating paste.

To make matters worse, all morning Jessica Finch kept inching her desk a little closer, a little closer to Judy.

"Is that the elbow that was in the paper?" Jessica asked.

Judy drew a mad face on her famous elbow and pointed it at Jessica.

"Hey, Judy? Want to come over to my house after school?" asked Jessica. "I could show you my glow-in-the-dark spelling posters."

"Can't," said Judy.

"Why not?"

"I have to feed Jaws, my Venus flytrap."

"How about tomorrow?"

"I feed it every day," said Judy.

"How about after you feed Jaws?" asked Jessica.

"Homework," said Judy.

The truth: by Friday Judy was almost bored enough to go to Jessica's. Rocky had to stay at his grandma's after school for a week because his mom was working late, and Frank could hardly do anything with a broken finger.

Too bad she had finished operating on all the hospital dolls so quickly. Making a cast was the best!

If only she could try making a bigger cast, on a human patient. But who? Stink would not let her near him with wet oogey newspaper.

Judy looked back at Jessica Finch. Maybe she did not look like a Pinch Face. Maybe she did not look like an aardwolf. Maybe she looked like . . . a doctor's dream. The perfect patient!

"Hey, Jessica," Judy asked, "how would you like to get your arm in a cast?"

"It's not broken," Jessica said.

"Who cares?" said Judy. "It's just for fun."

"Sure, I guess. Does this mean you'll come over? I can show you my spelling posters."

"How does today after school sound?" asked Judy.

❀   ❀   ❀

When Judy got to Jessica Finch's house, the two girls went up to Jessica's room. Judy looked around. All she could see were pigs. Pink pigs. Stuffed pigs. Piggy banks. A fuzzy piggy-face rug. Even Jessica's bed looked like a pig wearing a pink skirt.

"You like pigs!" said Judy.

"What was your first clue?" Jessica laughed in her hyena way.

Judy touched the spelling bee prize ribbons Jessica had hanging on the wall. Jessica showed Judy her scrapbook, with all the times her name had been in the paper.

"Wow," said Judy. "Did they ever spell your name wrong?"

"Once. Jessica Flinch!"

"Judy Muddy!" said Judy.

"Look! Here are all the spelling posters I made." Jessica pointed to the wall next to her bed.

"Hey, they're green. How come they're not pink too?"

"Because they glow in the dark. Wait." Jessica pulled down the shades and turned off the light.

The room lit up with glow-in-the-dark words. All the spelling words from Mr. Todd!

BICYCLE

ICICLE

BREADSICLE

POPSICLE

RECYCLE

MOTORCYCLE

"What's a breadsicle?" Judy asked. "Is that like pumpernickel?"

"Hey, you're good," said Jessica. "See, I make up fake words and play a game to see if I can fool myself. Want to play? Or we could play the pig game. Instead of dice you get to roll little plastic pigs."

"What about making a cast?" said Judy.

"You're not going to break my finger or anything, like you did to Frank, are you?"

"No! Besides, it was an accident," Judy said.

"Okay. So. What do we need?" asked Jessica.

"Newspaper. Water. Glue."

"This comes off, right?" said Jessica.

"Right," said Judy. *There must be some way to get it off*, she thought. "We have to let it dry first. Then we paint it."

"Can we paint it pink?" asked Jessica.

"Sure," Judy said. *Rare. A pink cast.*

"I'll go get some old newspapers," said Jessica.

When she came back, she said, "All I could find was today's, so let's hope my parents have already read it!"

Judy and Jessica tore the paper into strips. Judy could not wait to see the pink cast. This was her biggest operation yet!

Judy dipped paper strips into the sticky mixture and carefully placed them one by one on Jessica's arm.

"Ooh. It feels icky," said Jessica. "Are you sure this is going to work?"

Jessica was as bad as Stink. "Here," said Judy, handing Jessica more newspaper. "Tear up some more strips. I'm running out."

Jessica handed Judy a strip. At the top was the word PHANTOM. Jessica handed Judy another strip. STRIKES. A third. HOSPITAL.

"Stop!" said Judy. "Where's the rest of this story?" She peered at Jessica's arm. "Page B six. Where's page B six, huh?"

"Oh. I think I already ripped it up."

Judy tried to read Jessica's wet, oogey arm, but all she could make out were the

words *doll thief.* "What did it say?" she asked in a panic.

"Phantom strikes county hospital, or something."

"Or something, what?"

"I don't know. What's the big deal?"

Judy stood up suddenly, scattering paper strips everywhere. "I gotta go!"

"You what? Wait! My arm! You can't just . . . What about my pink cast?" But Judy was already out the door.

She, Judy Moody, Doll Thief, would be famous all right. For going to jail. Just like Stink said.

Judy Moody, Superhero

"Home already?" asked Mom. "How was Jessica's? Fun?"

"I . . . did you . . . where's . . . the . . . paper?" Judy asked, out of breath.

"Today's paper? Right here," said Dad, pushing it across the table toward Judy.

Judy flipped through the paper madly. But when she got to Section B, all she saw was a giant hole.

"Who cut up the paper? Stink?" she said,
shooting him her best stinging-caterpillar
eyebrow look.

"Oh, I did," said Dad. "Here, I tacked it
up right here on the fridge."

He read out loud:

**PHANTOM DOLL DOCTOR STRIKES
COUNTY HOSPITAL**

On Saturday, October 17, Grace Porter, a member
of the nursing staff at County General, noticed that
several of the dolls that had been donated to the
hospital for its Magic Playroom were missing.

"Funny coincidence," said Mom. "That
was the same day we took Frank to the
hospital!"

"Ha. Funny," said Judy, trying to smile.
Mom would not find it so funny when she
learned that her only daughter was an all-
out, true-blue, I-before-E thief.

Dad continued reading:

The missing dolls created quite a stir. Young patients
who use the Magic Playroom in the Children's Wing
spent days speculating as to the identity of the doll
thief.

"Isn't that where I found you two?" asked Mom. "The Magic Playroom?" Judy's mother sounded just like a detective. *Jail time.*

Curiously, a mysterious package was received a few days later, with all the dolls magically cleaned, scrubbed, fixed, or mended. Each one was tagged, dressed in a hospital gown, and had been properly "doctored" with fancy Band-Aids, slings, and casts.

Dad paused and said, "Hmm. Band-Aids." *Uh-oh*, thought Judy. *Evidence.*

A special doll with a once-broken heart was given to patient Laura Chumsky, who recently underwent the hospital's twenty-ninth heart transplant. On behalf of Laura Chumsky and all the young patients, the hospital staff would like to thank the anonymous donor, the Phantom Doll Doctor, for this kind contribution.

"It sounds like one of the superheroes in my comics!" Stink said.

"That's quite a story," said Dad, grinning.

"Let me see that," Judy said. She had to see it, had to read it, with her very own eyes. "Phantom Doll Doctor," she repeated, touching the words in the headline. "Rare!"

"What a thoughtful thing for someone to do," said Mom.

"Wish I'd thought of it," said Dad, tacking the article back up on the refrigerator with a pineapple magnet. There it was, front and center in the Moody Hall of Fame.

"Too bad," said Stink.

"What's too bad?" said Judy.

"I kind of wanted to see the inside of a jail."

"Hardee-har-har," said Judy, nervously glancing at her parents. But they were both grinning proudly. That's when Judy's brain began working on a brand-new Judy Moody idea.

She'd make a sign. Maybe set up shop in the garage. Get other kids to give her their broken dolls or old stuffed animals. Or she'd find some at yard sales. She would doctor them up and donate them to more sick kids in the Children's Wing at the hospital. Some could have Ace bandages, or fancy scars, or tubes for breathing. Maybe even an IV!

And it could all be in secret. The hospital would never know the identity of the Phantom Doll Doctor. The way nobody knew Superman was really Clark Kent, a nice, quiet reporter from the *Daily Planet*.

Rare!

For the first time in a long time, the once Judy Muddy felt more famous than an elbow.

She, Judy Moody, Phantom Doll Doctor, now felt as famous as Queen Elizabeth, as famous as George Washington, as famous as Superman.

Famouser!

Wouldn't Elizabeth Blackwell, First Woman Doctor, be proud!